Robert D. San Souci
·1995·

The Samurai's Daughter

A JAPANESE LEGEND RETOLD BY

Robert D. San Souci

PICTURES BY

Stephen T. Johnson

 Dial Books for Young Readers New York

Published by Dial Books for Young Readers
A Division of Penguin Books USA Inc.
375 Hudson Street · New York, New York 10014

Design by Atha Tehon
Printed in the U.S.A.
First Edition
3 4 5 6 7 8 9 10

Library of Congress Cataloging in Publication Data
San Souci, Robert D.
The samurai's daughter/retold from a
Japanese legend by Robert D. San Souci;
pictures by Stephen T. Johnson.
p.   cm.
Adaptation of: A story of Oki Islands.
Summary: A Japanese folktale about the brave
daughter of a samurai warrior and her journey to be reunited
with her exiled father.
ISBN 0-8037-1135-2 (trade) — ISBN 0-8037-1136-0 (lib. bdg.)
[1. Folklore — Japan.] I. Johnson, Stephen, 1964–   ill.
II. Story of Oki Islands. III. Title.
PZ8.1.S227Sam 1992 398.2 — dc20 [E] 91-15585 CIP AC

The full-color paintings were created with pastels.
The artwork was scanner-separated and reproduced as
red, blue, yellow, and black halftones.

For Nancy Bronstein, whose friendship, assistance,
and encouragement are such valuable resources to me

R. S. S.

For Doug and Hiromi and their son, Howie-Chan

S. T. J.

This tale is set in medieval Japan during the Kamakura Period (1185–1333). Primary sources include "A Story of Oki Islands" in Ancient Tales and Folklore of Japan *(1908) by Richard Gordon-Smith, and an adaptation published as "The Slaughter of the Sea Serpent" in* Myths and Legends of Japan *(1912) by F. Hadland Davis. In his introduction to the earlier work Gordon-Smith comments, "The stories in this volume are transcribed from voluminous illustrated diaries which have been kept by me for some twenty years spent in travel and in sport in many lands—the last nine of them almost entirely in Japan, while collecting subjects of natural history for the British Museum [and] trawling and dredging in the Inland Sea [site of the Oki Islands]."*

A variety of collateral sources provided insight into the history and culture of the period; the geography of Shima province on Japan's west coast and situation of the Oki Islands; matters political, military, and religious; and the remarkable feats of the diving women, whose time-honored occupation continues to draw great numbers of tourists to Shima province.

Long ago on the east coast of Japan there lived a noble *samurai*, a knight, who spent much of his time traveling in the service of Japan's ruler. A widower, he devoted the rest of his time to raising his beautiful daughter Tokoyo.

Though she was a girl, her father schooled her in the samurai virtues of courage, discipline, and endurance; he taught her a warrior's duty to protect the weak. When she was five, he trained her to shoot a bow and arrow, and to ride a horse.

But when she grew older, her father decided that she ought to learn to be more ladylike. Teachers gave her lessons in proper manners and dress, composing poems, dancing, and playing the *biwa,* a lute.

To her nurse, Kuma, the girl complained, "How I wish I could live as a boy! They go hawking; they compete for honors in horsemanship and archery."

Kuma scolded Tokoyo good-naturedly, "Those are foolish things for a young woman to wish."

But Tokoyo seized any chance to prove herself as strong and brave as any true samurai. Despite her noble birth, she spent much time with the *amas,* women divers. Women were better able than men to withstand cold water and hold more air in their lungs, and so they harvested abalone, pearl oysters, and other shellfish.

Tokoyo loved rowing out in the small boats in the sunlit mornings, then diving down, knife in hand, to pry reluctant oysters and abalone from the rocks, and fill the basket strapped to her back.

Sometimes she found big shells lined with lustrous mother-of-pearl that could be polished and cut into dishes and bowls. But there was also danger: Once a shark swam slowly beneath the boats while Tokoyo hid behind a rock. Just when she felt her lungs would burst, the shark returned to the open sea.

One spring day when Tokoyo was eighteen, she stood on the shore with her friends, sorting the morning's catch, cleaning abalone shells, and setting the meat to dry on bamboo mats.

She was surprised to see her father coming across the beach toward her in his court robes and headdress of stiff black cloth, with a soldier on either side.

Happily Tokoyo ran to him crying, "Father, I thought you would be away for many days yet."

The man smiled sadly. "I have displeased our ruler. He has banished me to the Oki Islands, in the western sea beyond the mountains."

"But you are his most loyal knight!" Tokoyo protested.

"For a long time a strange disorder has plagued his mind," answered her father. "He fears even his most devoted knights and counselors. He has banished others before me. If the illness leaves him, he will realize his mistake. But he is my lord. I am his faithful samurai. I must do as he commands."

Parent and child clung to each other for the last time. For her father's sake, because she was the daughter of a samurai, Tokoyo tried to hide her grief. But tears streamed down her face, though neither she nor her father would acknowledge them.

When the soldiers took her father away, she angrily wiped away the tears that had betrayed her.

For weeks Tokoyo paced behind the rice-paper walls of her house, weeping from morning till night, hiding her face in the sleeve of her *kimono,* robe.

By summer, unable to bear being parted from her father any longer, she decided to join him in his exile. I am the daughter of a samurai, she thought, I must go where loyalty requires, and trust that my courage will carry me there.

On the night before Tokoyo left, Kuma gave her a tiny bamboo cage in which a cricket sang.

"He sounds so happy!" the girl exclaimed, surprised that there could be any happiness left in the world.

"This will bring you luck," said the old woman.

"I will return one day," said Tokoyo, deeply touched. She hugged her old servant, adding, "I will find a way to bring my father home, and return honor to our house."

She planned to travel alone, dressed as a peasant in wooden clogs, *geta;* a shaggy cape of straw, a *mino,* that would protect her from heat or cold; and a peaked straw hat. She also took her cricket, a dagger that had belonged to one of her ancestors, and a bag of dried fish.

The next day she set out across the mountains to the shore of the western sea. From there she would cross to the Oki Islands, where her father lived in exile.

Her journey proved difficult. Twice she had to hide from bandits who prowled the high roads. But her courage, the hope of seeing her father, and the cricket's tireless song helped keep her spirits high.

Eventually she reached a small fishing village on the seashore. But when she asked the people to ferry her across to the islands, they refused.

"The ruler has forbidden anyone to go there without his permission," said one man with a shrug.

"The wind and waves make it dangerous for small boats, even in summer," a woman added.

"The ghost of a sunken warship haunts those waters," said a very old fisherman.

"Still I must go," said Tokoyo.

She spent the last of her money to buy a light, swift boat to carry her across the water to the island where her father was. The fisher folk shook their heads, doubting that she would reach the island of exiles, which they told her was marked by a rock shaped like a skull.

At dawn the young woman set out across the sea. Standing in the boat, she moved the oars steadily back-and-forth, as the amas, the diving women, had taught her. Under her straw mino the cricket sang his song.

Pausing only briefly to rest, she sculled her boat until darkness fell. The full moon cast a shimmer of light across the waves like a silver dragon. Though weary, Tokoyo felt sure that she would soon be reunited with her father.

Suddenly her cricket stopped singing. The young woman saw a ghostly white warship rushing silently toward her across the waves. Huge white sails, filled with no earthly wind, and banks of rising and falling oars drove it ever closer.

Knowing she could not outrun the ghost-ship, Tokoyo stood bravely facing her doom. "I am the daughter of a samurai!" she shouted.

Now ghostly warriors leaned over the rails, their pale hands reaching for her. She raised an oar to do battle. But the horrible ship washed over her like chill mist, then vanished, leaving her alone on the water.

A short time later she reached the Oki Islands. In the moonlight she saw the nearest island was marked with a huge gray rock shaped like a skull. Tokoyo knew that she had reached her destination.

Filled with fresh hope, the young woman beached her boat on a rocky cape near a grove of pine trees. There she heard clapping and bitter sobbing.

Leaving her cricket cage under her folded mino, she pushed quietly through the pines until she came to the tip of the little point of land. There she saw a sad-faced old man dressed in a priest's white robes and a pretty girl of fifteen or so, also wearing white, who was weeping. The girl's tears touched Tokoyo as a woman and as a samurai who was duty-bound to help the helpless.

The priest clapped again to catch the ears of the gods in heaven, then he said a prayer. At last he led the sobbing girl to the rocky seawall. He was about to push her into the water, when Tokoyo jumped out and pulled the girl back.

The old man looked surprised, but not angry. "From your actions I guess that you are a stranger to our island. Otherwise you would know that this sad duty makes me and all of the people here very unhappy.

"We are cursed with an evil demon, a great white serpent, who lives at the bottom of the sea. Every year he demands the sacrifice of a young girl or boy. If we refuse, he becomes angry and raises storms that drown our fishermen."

Tokoyo said, "Let this child go, oh Priest! I am the daughter of a samurai, and duty demands that I help the weak. I ask you to let me take the place of this unhappy girl."

When the old man agreed, Tokoyo walked bravely to the water's edge, gripped her dagger between her teeth, and dived into the sea.

Down, down she swam until she reached the dark mouth of a cave surrounded with glowing abalone shells and pearls. By their light she discovered what appeared to be a small, seated man. But when she swam close, Tokoyo found that it was instead a waterlogged wooden statue of the ruler who had exiled her father.

Brilliant white light suddenly boiled out of the cave, and Tokoyo beheld a horrible creature, writhing like a snake, uncoiling its vast length. Its back was covered with hard, shining scales, though its pale underside seemed soft and unprotected. The serpent's eyes blazed with cold fire as it swam straight at her, propelled like a centipede by dozens of short legs.

She knew that this was the evil sea-demon, thinking her his next victim. Faster he came, jaws gaping, but Tokoyo waited until the last instant. Then she darted sideways, putting out his right eye. Stunned, the wounded creature fled back to its cave, while Tokoyo swam to the surface to gasp for fresh air.

She had barely filled her lungs, when the sea serpent exploded from the nearby waves. He lunged for her, roaring; but she dove deep, and eluded his deadly teeth.

The girl turned and twisted through the water, narrowly avoiding the serpent who was slowed by the wound she had given him.

Tokoyo broke the surface again, gasping for air, then plunged away from the demon who was almost upon her. She wheeled about quickly and attacked him from his blind side. This time she struck the monster to the heart through his soft underbelly.

Coiling and uncoiling, the fatally wounded serpent sank down and slowly expired near the mouth of his cave. With a great effort Tokoyo managed to draw the monster's body onto the shore, while the priest and young girl watched in amazement.

Then Tokoyo brought up the wooden statue of the Japanese ruler, and set it on a rock to dry. Then she, the priest, and the girl went to the nearby village to tell what had happened.

There Tokoyo was embraced by her father.

"My daughter," he said, "your loyalty and courage make me very happy and do great honor to our family."

"Let me stay with you, and I will be content," she said. "If we cannot go home, we will build a life here."

However, they soon discovered that the wooden statue Tokoyo rescued had been carved and cursed by a man that the ruler had banished to the island years before. When hurled into the sea, the statue had summoned the sea serpent, and had caused the distant ruler's madness.

The minute the statue was pulled from the water, the ruler's mind grew sound. When word reached him of what Tokoyo had done, he ordered the samurai and his brave daughter to be returned home, and heaped with many honors. There they enjoyed peace and prosperity for the rest of their lives.